MR. WOLF'S CLASS

FIELD TRIP

ARON NELS STEINKE

Graphix AN IMPRINT OF SCHOLASTIC

For Ariel

Library of Congress Control Number: 2019950318

ISBN 978-1-338-61764-1 (hardcover)
ISBN 978-1-338-61763-4 (paperback)

10 9 8 7 6 5 4 3 2 1   20 21 22 23 24

Printed in Heshan, China   62
First edition, October 2020

Edited by Cassandra Pelham Fulton
Book design by Phil Falco
Publisher: David Saylor

7

CHAPTER ONE
The Silent Treatment

SLAM

HA! HA!

FWOMP

OUCH!

ABDI! HENRY!

CUT IT OUT!

SORRY!

YEAH, SORRY.

THANK YOU.

OKAY, EVERYONE, PLEASE LISTEN AS I CALL YOUR NAME AND YOUR CABIN GROUP ASSIGNMENT.

THE LAST GROUP IS COMPRISED OF ABDI, HENRY, NOAH, ME...

SAMPSON, AND OSCAR.

BUT, MR. WOLF... OSCAR ISN'T HERE YET.

WE'LL GIVE HIM A FEW MORE MINUTES, BUT THEN WE'LL HAVE TO BE ON OUR WAY.

COME SIT WITH ME, PENNY.

OSCAR, WHERE ARE YOU?!

ZELWOOD S

THAT'S FINE, PENNY. GO AHEAD. YOU CAN SIT WITH LOLA.

HI, AZIZA. CAN I TALK WITH YOU FOR A MINUTE?

MARGOT, RANDY, DO EITHER OF YOU KNOW WHY AZIZA IS SO UPSET? SHE DOESN'T WANT TO TELL ME ABOUT IT.

WELL, I WAS TRYING TO GET HER TO COME SIT WITH US, BUT SHE JUST IGNORED ME. I DON'T KNOW WHAT'S GOING ON.

RANDY, DO YOU KNOW WHAT'S GOING ON?

WELL, SORT OF...WE WERE HAVING A SLEEPOVER AT MY HOUSE THIS WEEKEND, BUT IT DIDN'T TURN OUT SO GREAT.

WE KIND OF HAD A LITTLE DISAGREEMENT, AND I GUESS SHE'S STILL MAD AT ME.

HMM. MAYBE SHE JUST NEEDS SOME TIME AND SOME SPACE.

MR. WOLF, TRAFFIC IS GOING TO GET WORSE THE LONGER WE WAIT.

WE SHOULD GET GOING.

YOU'RE RIGHT. WE NEED TO LEAVE NOW.

IT'S LATE.

HERE WE GO, EVERYONE. NEXT STOP, BATTLE AX CREEK!

ERR-VROOM

IT'S TOO BAD OSCAR'S GOING TO MISS THIS TRIP.

ELWOOD S

RUMBLE VROOOOM

HAZELTON THE MUSICAL

PLAY

AND NOW A PLURAL NOUN.

CHAPTER TWO

Are We There Yet?

SEE YOU TOMORROW AFTERNOON. LISTEN TO YOUR TEACHER, BOBBY.

STOP

BYE. THANK YOU SO MUCH.

BYE, DAD!

BYE, BUS DRIVER MAN.

REVERSE

VROOOM

GRAB YOUR LUNCHES, EVERYONE. TIME TO EAT.

MAKE SURE YOU USE THE BATHROOM IF YOU NEED TO GO.

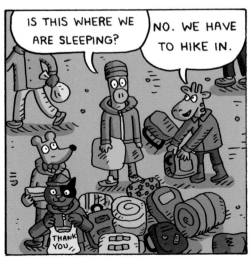

IS THIS WHERE WE ARE SLEEPING?

NO. WE HAVE TO HIKE IN.

THANK YOU

SO HUNGRY!

NOM NOM NOM

WANT SOME SPICY CHIPS, AZIZA? YUMMY! YOUR FAVORITE.

NO, THANK YOU.

HOT

CHOMP

GLUG GLUG

PUT YOUR TRASH IN THE TRASH CAN WHEN YOU ARE FINISHED.

TOSS

WE WANT TO LEAVE THIS PLACE CLEANER THAN IT WAS WHEN WE GOT HERE.

DROP

* TOO MUCH INFORMATION

YES, PENNY?

DO I HAVE TO GO TO THE BATHROOM?

LOUD!

BYE, SLEEPING BAGS AND PILLOWS.

ALL YOURS, JOHNNY.

P.U.!

I'VE SMELLED WORSE.

IT'S JUST A STINKY HOLE IN THE GROUND.

DO NOT PUT TRASH IN TOILET

BUZZ

...

NEVER MIND. THAT IS DISGUSTING!

AND YOU ARE GOING TO GET A CHANCE TO COME UP WITH YOUR OWN CAMP NAME LATER TODAY.

≷WHISPER≷

≷WHISPER≷

A QUESTION. YES?

IF HUCKLEBERRY IS YOUR CAMP NAME, THEN WHAT IS YOUR REAL NAME?

I WON'T TELL, BUT YOU CAN GUESS. YOU ONLY GET THREE GUESSES APIECE.

OOH!

AHH!

WHAT DO WE WIN IF WE GUESS RIGHT?

HMM...

I'M NOT SURE YET, BUT I'M GOING TO GIVE THIS YOUNG LADY SOMETHING.

ME?

ME?

WHEN YOU COMPLETE AN ACTIVITY, YOU CAN EARN BEADS. I ALSO GIVE THEM OUT ON SPECIAL OCCASIONS LIKE THIS.

GLINT

HERE YOU GO. THANK YOU FOR BEING A GOOD LISTENER AND FOR RAISING YOUR HAND TO ASK YOUR QUESTION.

SAVE IT FOR WHEN WE MAKE NECKLACES.

SEE, MR. WOLF. I AM LISTENING.

OOH!

IS YOUR NAME IRENE?

NO.

MICHELLE?

NO.

FLORENCE?

AND NO.

YOU'RE OUT OF GUESSES.

DON'T EVERYBODY GUESS ALL AT ONCE. TAKE YOUR TIME. I'LL BE OFFERING CLUES THROUGHOUT YOUR STAY, BUT YOU MUST LISTEN CLOSELY FOR THEM.

ONWARD. FOLLOW ME.

TODAY, WE ARE GOING TO HIKE TO THE GHOST TOWN OF BATTLE AX CREEK.

DID SHE SAY GHOST TOWN?!

A GHOST TOWN IS WHAT WE CALL A PLACE THAT USED TO HAVE LOTS OF PEOPLE LIVING THERE BUT DOESN'T ANYMORE.

BATTLE AX CREEK WAS ONCE A THRIVING MINING TOWN.

PEOPLE CAME FROM ALL OVER TO MINE FOR PRECIOUS METALS. THEN THEY SUFFERED A SERIES OF BAD ACCIDENTS.

AFTER SEVERAL COLLAPSED MINES, TWO TRAIN DERAILMENTS, AND A BLIZZARD, ONE AFTER ANOTHER, THE MINERS ALL LEFT.

THAT'S HOW IT BECAME A GHOST TOWN. BUT I'LL TELL YOU MORE ABOUT THAT LATER.

LET'S GET A MOVE ON.

HERE WE HAVE ONE OF THE OLDEST DOUGLAS FIR TREES IN THE WORLD.

ANYONE CARE TO GUESS HOW OLD IT IS?

TWO HUNDRED YEARS OLD?

OLDER.

THREE HUNDRED?

MUCH OLDER.

EIGHT HUNDRED?

OLDER STILL.

ONE THOUSAND.

PRETTY CLOSE. WE ESTIMATE THAT THIS TREE IS CLOSE TO ELEVEN HUNDRED YEARS OLD.

THERE AREN'T A LOT OF OLD-GROWTH FORESTS LIKE THIS LEFT AROUND HERE.

THAT'S WHY WE NEED TO PROTECT THE ONES WE HAVE LEFT.

ABOUT THIRTY YEARS AGO THEY HAD PLANS TO LOG AND CLEAR-CUT THIS ENTIRE FOREST.

BUT CONSERVATIONISTS AND ENVIRONMENTAL GROUPS CAME TOGETHER TO MAKE A PLAN TO PROTECT ALL THE PLANTS AND ANIMALS THAT LIVE HERE.

AFTER A LOT OF VERY HARD WORK THEY WERE SUCCESSFUL...

AND NOW THERE IS A LAW PROTECTING THIS FOREST SO YOU AND I CAN ENJOY IT.

MAYBE ONE DAY YOU'LL BRING YOUR KIDS AND GRANDKIDS HERE TO SHOW THEM HOW SPECIAL THIS PLACE IS.

GIGGLE

WHOA!

!

WHAT?!

OUR KIDS?

DON'T YOU MEAN IF WE HAVE KIDS?

GOSH!

YOU ARE RIGHT. IF YOU HAVE KIDS.

AND OVER HERE WE HAVE AN ABANDONED MINE SHAFT.

IT STARTED OUT AS A GOLD MINE.

GOLD!

BUT THEY DIDN'T FIND MUCH GOLD SO THEY GAVE UP.

AW!

THERE WAS NO JOY TO BE FOUND IN THERE.

41

THAT'S BECAUSE FOR SOME REASON WE DON'T REALLY TALK AT SCHOOL.

BUT WE HANG OUT AFTER SCHOOL AND ON MOST WEEKENDS.

MAYBE WE DON'T TALK IN SCHOOL BECAUSE WE HAVE DIFFERENT FRIENDS IN CLASS. LIKE, SHE'S GOT AZIZA AND RANDY, AND THEN YOU'RE MY BEST FRIEND.

BUT I DO THINK OF MARGOT AS ONE OF MY GOOD FRIENDS. I REALLY LIKE HER.

DOES THAT MEAN YOU LIKE HER, LIKE HER?

WHAT DID I SAY?

HUCKLEBERRY, WHAT ARE THESE BERRIES CALLED?

HMMM...LET'S SEE. AHA!

ANYONE KNOW WHAT THEY ARE CALLED?

DON'T EAT IT!

TART!

JUST THINK, IT'S MY FAVORITE KIND OF BERRY.

OOH!

HUCKLEBERRIES?

BINGO! *VACCINIUM PARVIFOLIUM*. RED HUCKLEBERRY.

I'M SURPRISED TO SEE ANY LEFT. IT'S VERY LATE IN THE SEASON.

THEY'RE DELICIOUS! ESPECIALLY IN A PIE.

TOLD YA.

CAN YOU REALLY EAT THEM?

SURE CAN.

DO YOU SEE HOW THE BUSH IS GROWING OUT OF THAT OLD CEDAR STUMP? DEAD TREES SUPPORT NEW LIFE.

A LONG TIME AGO, A BIRD OR MAMMAL MUST HAVE EATEN A BERRY FROM ANOTHER BUSH.

THEN, WHEN THE ANIMAL POOPED, THE BERRY SEEDS GOT DEPOSITED HERE. THE DEAD TREE ACTED AS FERTILIZER...YES, POOP IS FUNNY!

SNORT SNICKER

HAW! HAW!

LET'S KEEP MOVING. WE'VE GOT A LOT OF GROUND TO COVER.

WHEN ARE WE GONNA BE THERE?

YOU CAN DO IT, PENNY!

UGH! I'M JUST SO TIRED OF WALKING.

IT FEELS LIKE WE'VE BEEN WALKING FOR DAYS AND DAYS!

COME ON, PENNY. WE'RE ALMOST THERE.

ARE YOU SURE?

SURE. IT'S PROBABLY JUST RIGHT AROUND THE CORNER.

FWOMP

48

CHAPTER THREE
New Friends

50

SSSSL...HUH?!

WHOA!

WHAT DAY IS IT? WHERE AM I? WHAT AM I DOING HERE?

I MUST HAVE PASSED OUT.

HOW ARE YOU FEELING, AZIZA? DID YOU GET SOME SLEEP? YOU MUST HAVE BEEN EXHAUSTED.

...

GO ON AND FIND YOUR FRIENDS. EVERYONE IS PLAYING IN THE MEADOW.

OKAY. THANK YOU, GENEVIEVE.

CALL ME GI-GI.

THEY'RE PLAYING WITH KIDS FROM ANOTHER SCHOOL?

THEY MADE NEW FRIENDS WHILE I WAS ASLEEP!

OH NO! WHAT IF THEY DON'T WANT ME AS A FRIEND ANYMORE?

WHAT IF I'VE BEEN REPLACED?

HI, AZIZA.

ZI-ZI...

55

WHOA!

THAT WAS AMAZING!

LAST CALL FOR CLOVERDALE FIFTH GRADERS...

OOPS! I'VE GOTTA GO!

I'M AZIZA. WHAT'S YOUR NAME?

IT'S Navan

?

CHAPTER FOUR
Camp Names

HOWDY, YA'LL. MY NAME IS OX. OUR FIRST ACTIVITY IS TO PICK OUT A CAMP NAME AND MAKE A NAME BADGE LIKE THE ONE I'M WEARING. YOU'LL FIND ALL THE SUPPLIES YOU'LL NEED IN FRONT OF YOU. LET'S GET STARTED.

ERRR!

THIS IS SO FRUSTRATING!

UGH! I GIVE UP!

YOU DON'T KNOW HOW TO TIE A BOW?

BUT YOU WEAR SHOES WITH LACES. DOES YOUR MOM TIE THEM FOR YOU OR SOMETHING?

YEAH AND THEN I NEVER UNTIE THEM. AND WHEN I WANT TO PUT THEM ON AGAIN, I JUST SHOVE MY FEET INSIDE.

HA! HA!

ALL RIGHT, I'LL TEACH YOU HOW. JUST DO WHAT I DO.

UNTIE

CROSS.

IT JUST TAKES PRACTICE. YOU'LL GET IT.

LOOKS LIKE SWORD FERN NEEDS A LITTLE HELP.

THANK YOU.

YOU'LL NEVER LEARN HOW TO DO IT IF YOU KEEP LETTING OTHER PEOPLE DO IT FOR YOU.

GURGLE

ONE MORE MINUTE UNTIL WE SHARE OUR NAMES.

EXCUSE ME, OX, I NEED TO FIND A TOILET.

BRB!*

DART

*BE RIGHT BACK

63

I'LL BEGIN. MY REAL NAME IS JESSICA AND MY CAMP NAME IS OX.

HI. MY REAL NAME IS MARGOT AND MY CAMP NAME IS CLOVER.

MY REAL NAME IS RANDY AND MY CAMP NAME IS... BANANA SLUG!

REALLY?

BANANA SLUGS ARE BEAUTIFUL CREATURES. I'VE NEVER MET ONE I DIDN'T LIKE.

MY REAL NAME IS LOLA AND MY CAMP NAME IS HEMLOCK.

MY REAL NAME IS PENNY AND MY CAMP NAME IS BUMBLEBEE.

MY REAL NAME IS BOBBY AND MY CAMP NAME IS WOLVERINE.

MY REAL NAME IS STEWART AND MY CAMP NAME IS OXALIS.

MY REAL NAME IS OLIVER AND MY CAMP NAME IS BLACKBERRY.

MY REAL NAME IS MOLLY AND MY CAMP NAME IS DANDELION. THAT MEANS "LION'S TOOTH" IN FRENCH.

MY REAL NAME IS NOAH AND MY CAMP NAME IS LI'L CRAWDAD.

MY REAL NAME IS MIGUEL LOUIS SANTIAGO RIVERA AND MY CAMP NAME IS THUNDER EGG!

MY REAL NAME IS LIZZY AND MY CAMP NAME IS RIVER.

MY REAL NAME IS SAMPSON AND MY CAMP NAME IS BADGER.

MY REAL NAME IS ABDI AND MY CAMP NAME IS SCORPION.

MY REAL NAME IS HENRY AND MY CAMP NAME IS RATTLE-SNAKE.

MY REAL NAME IS JOHNNY AND MY CAMP NAME IS ROBIN HOOD!

I'M BACK!

JUST IN TIME. WE'RE SHARING OUR CAMP NAMES.

OX

OKAY, MY REAL NAME IS OSCAR AND MY CAMP NAME IS SWORD FERN.

Sword Fern

ADULTS?

I'M SAMPSON'S MOM, GENEVIEVE, AND MY CAMP NAME IS ELDERBERRY.

Elder Berry

HI, I'M ROBIN HOOD'S UNCLE FRED. MY CAMP NAME IS RANGER.

Ranger

I'M MOLLY'S MOM, THU, AND MY CAMP NAME IS RHUBARB.

Rhubarb

AND, MR. FOX, WHAT IS YOUR CAMP NAME?

?!

OX

GO AHEAD, WE'RE LISTENING.

WELL, MY REAL NAME IS AZIZA AND MY FRIENDS CALL ME ZI-ZI...

BUT I JUST CAN'T THINK OF A GOOD CAMP NAME. NOTHING I COME UP WITH FEELS RIGHT.

THAT'S NOT A PROBLEM, AZIZA. YOU CAN TAKE YOUR TIME. WE'LL JUST USE YOUR REAL NAME UNTIL THEN.

FOLLOW ME. WE'VE GOT LOTS OF ACTIVITIES TO DO TODAY.

I'VE GOT TO THINK OF A GOOD NAME.

FOREST SHELTERS

CABINS

MEADOW

70

FIRST ACTIVITY: A VISIT TO THE POWER HOUSE

HERE IS WHERE WE GET MOST OF OUR ELECTRICITY.

THE FORCE OF THE FALLING WATER TURNS THE BLADES OF THE TURBINES.

S H H H H H

THE TURBINES SPIN MAGNETS AROUND BUNDLES OF COPPER WIRES TO GENERATE ELECTRICITY.

TRANSFORMER

GENERATOR

H_2O IN

TURBINE

SILT

H_2O OUT

YOU HAVE SOLAR POWER, TOO, RIGHT?

GOOD OBSERVATION, AZIZA. THANKS FOR POINTING THAT OUT.

THESE ROOFTOP SOLAR PANELS ARE BUSY GENERATING ENERGY, EVEN ON CLOUDY DAYS.

STAFF

OF COURSE, IT'S BEST ON SUNNY DAYS LIKE TODAY.

IS SUNNY YOUR NAME?

NO, BUT GOOD GUESS.

HUCKLE-BERRY!

SAY GOOD-BYE TO OX. SHE'S GOING TO JOIN THE OTHER GROUP WHILE I SHOW YOU SOMETHING REALLY HOT.

BYE!

SEE YOU SOON.

OX

THIS SUPER-HOT WATER COMES FROM DEEP IN THE EARTH WHERE IT'S HEATED BY HOT AND MOLTEN ROCK. WE USE THIS WATER TO KEEP OUR CABINS TOASTY.

GEOTHERMAL.

STINKY!

MMM... SMELLS GOOD!

BUBB

BUBBLE

BUBB

WHY DOES IT SMELL LIKE FARTS?

THAT'S HYDROGEN SULFIDE GAS.

MORE LIKE ROTTEN EGGS.

72

SECOND ACTIVITY: PLANT IDENTIFICATION SCAVENGER HUNT

I THINK THIS IS ONE.

Draw a sword Fern

WESTERN HEMLOCK SEED CONE: CHECK!

IT'S SO TINY!

HERE'S A DECOMPOSING BIGLEAF MAPLE LEAF.

DOUGLAS FIR SEED CONE

SEE HOW IT LOOKS LIKE LITTLE RAT LEGS AND TAIL?

RED ALDER BARK IS SMOOTH.

AND MOSSY.

WESTERN RED CEDAR LEAVES SMELL HEAVENLY.

MMM.

SNIFF

INHALE

NEXT: BUILD A SHELTER

CRASH

ARE WE STILL FRIENDS?

74

MR. WOLF, IT'S NOT FAIR! THEY'RE FIFTH GRADERS! THEY'RE OLDER THAN US.

SURE, BUT WE HAD MORE PEOPLE THAN THEY DID.

I THINK YOU WERE PRETTY EVENLY MATCHED.

CAN WE HAVE A REMATCH? PLEASE?

HMM.

YEAH!

TELL YOU WHAT, WE'VE GOT FIFTEEN MINUTES OF FREE TIME. IF YOU AND YOUR FRIENDS WANT TO PLAY AGAIN, BE MY GUEST.

NO WAY!

CHAPTER FIVE

Out of Bounds

OOOH! THE SKY WORLD SERIES! I THOUGHT I'D READ THEM ALL, BUT I'VE NEVER SEEN THIS ONE BEFORE.

WAIT A SECOND. IS THIS A COMIC BOOK?

YEAH, THEY'RE ADAPTING THE WHOLE SERIES INTO GRAPHIC NOVELS. THIS IS BOOK TWO.

IT'S INTERESTING TO SEE WHAT CHANGES AND WHAT STAYS THE SAME.

YAWN

DO YOU LIKE THE MUSIC FROM *HAZELTON*?

I DON'T KNOW WHAT THAT IS.

HERE. YOU'VE GOT TO LISTEN.

ALEXANDER HAZELTON WAS A FOUNDING FATHER AND THEY MADE A HIP-HOP MUSICAL ABOUT HIS LIFE CALLED *HAZELTON.*

RANDY, MARGOT, AND I ARE OBSESSED!

SHE'S AT THE BEST PART!

HA! HA!

HEE! HEE!

YEAH!

SWAY BOB

GOOD, RIGHT?

I LIKE IT.

THE LYRICS ARE HYSTERICAL.

SO, WHO'RE MARGOT AND RANDY?

THEY'RE MY BEST FRIENDS.

BUT I'M SORT OF TAKING A BREAK FROM THEM RIGHT NOW.

ACTUALLY, I'M ONLY REALLY MAD AT RANDY. MARGOT HAS NOTHING TO DO WITH IT.

I'M READY TO FORGIVE RANDY, BUT I WISH SHE'D APOLOGIZE FIRST.

WHY AREN'T YOU HANGING OUT WITH ANYONE FROM YOUR SCHOOL?

...

NOBODY IN MY CLASS WANTS TO BE MY FRIEND. THEY ALL THINK I'M WEIRD OR SOMETHING.

AND I'VE BEEN IN THE SAME CLASS WITH THEM SINCE KINDERGARTEN.

NO FRIENDS?!

YIKES!

IF YOU DON'T HAVE ANY FRIENDS, WHAT DO YOU DO AT RECESS?

I DON'T REALLY LIKE CHASING OR BALL GAMES, SO I USED TO JUST WALK AROUND AND MAKE OBSERVATIONS.

LIKE OSCAR DOES SOME-TIMES.

AND THEN I NOTICED THAT THERE WAS TRASH ALL OVER THE PLAYGROUND. THERE WERE CHIP BAGS, BAR WRAPPERS, AND PLASTIC WATER BOTTLES.

SO I STARTED PICKING IT UP.

AFTER THAT I NOTICED THAT THERE WERE SOME OLD GARDEN BEDS WITH NOTHING IN THEM.

MY TEACHER GAVE ME PERMISSION TO START A VEGETABLE GARDEN. THEN THE KINDERGARTEN CLASS BEGAN HELPING ME WATER, WEED, AND PLANT SEEDS.

KINDERGARTNERS ARE ADORABLE.

RIGHT NOW WE'RE HARVESTING SQUASH, GARLIC, AND ONIONS. I'M ALSO PLANTING KALE.

I'M TRYING TO GET THE SCHOOL TO PUT IN A GREENHOUSE SO WE CAN GROW FOOD FOR SCHOOL LUNCHES.

THEY EVEN LET ME BUILD A CHICKEN COOP. WE'VE GOT A FEW HENS THAT WANDER AROUND AND I TALK TO THEM AND FEED THEM.

FUN!

SO THAT'S WHAT I MOSTLY DO AT RECESS NOW. I CALL IT ECOLOGY CLUB.

THAT'S SO COOL! I LOVE IT!

I'VE NOTICED TRASH ON OUR PLAYGROUND, TOO. IT'S DISGUSTING.

OUR CUSTODIAN PICKS IT UP SOMETIMES, BUT HE CAN'T GET IT ALL.

PLASTIC LITTER ON THE GROUND CAN GET WASHED INTO THE STORM DRAINS.

THEN THE STORM DRAINS CARRY THE TRASH INTO THE RIVERS AND THEN THE OCEAN.

AND IF IT'S MADE OF PLASTIC, IT CAN BREAK DOWN INTO ITTY-BITTY MICROPLASTIC. FISH AND WHALES MAY THINK IT'S FOOD AND EAT IT.

AND IF THEY EAT ENOUGH OF IT THEY COULD DIE.

MAYBE I'LL START MY OWN ECOLOGY CLUB AT HAZELWOOD.

REALLY?!

YEAH! YOU'VE INSPIRED ME.

WE'LL CLEAN UP THE PLAYGROUND, START A GARDEN, AND GET CHICKENS, TOO! I BET RANDY WOULD LOVE IT. SHE'D GET THE WHOLE SCHOOL EXCITED TO JOIN.

ECOLOGY CLUB IS GOING TO BE THE BEST CLUB EVER!

HI, PENNY. HOW'S IT GOING?

MR. WOLF, WHEN IS THIS DAY GOING TO END?

HMM. IT HAS BEEN QUITE A LONG DAY. IF THIS WERE A REGULAR SCHOOL DAY, YOU WOULD BE HOME BY NOW.

I THINK WE HAVE ONE MORE ACTIVITY, THEN DINNER. AFTER THAT IT'LL BE TIME FOR BED.

I COULD READ A BOOK WITH YOU. OR YOU COULD SEE WHAT THEY'RE BUILDING OVER THERE.

Adventure Zone

Adventure Zone

CAN YOU READ WITH ME? IF I HELP THEM BUILD WITH WOOD, I'M AFRAID I'LL GET A SPLINTER.

CHAPTER SIX
No Dancing

ALL RIGHT, EVERYONE, WE'RE GOING TO LEARN THE VIRGINIA REEL!

GO FIND A DANCE PARTNER.

THIS SOUNDS LIKE FUN.

I'LL ASK ABDI.

THIS DANCE IS SURE TO BRING YOU LOTS OF JOY!

DID SHE SAY DANCE?!

AZIZA, DO YOU WANT TO BE MY PARTNER?

OKAY!

I CAN'T! I WON'T! I'M NOT DANCING!

99

CHAPTER SEVEN
The Headless Miner

STRIKE

SIZZLE

FORM A LINE BEHIND A STOVE. ONE AT A TIME, PLEASE.

VEGGIE BURGERS OVER HERE.

MEAT BOOGERS, OVER HERE.

BOOGERS!

SQUIRT

MR. WOLF, YOU'RE HAVING A VEGGIE BURGER?

NOD

YEP.

WELCOME, RATTLESNAKE.

CHEW

SKOOOO

SO, ABDI, I KNOW YOU LIKE TO PLAY SOCCER, BUT WHAT ELSE DO YOU LIKE TO DO?

VIDEO GAMES.

LET'S SEE WHO CAN EAT THE MOST. WHAT DO YOU SAY, RATTLESNAKE? PITCHFORK'S ALREADY ON HIS THIRD.

SIZZLE

TOSS

COMPOST

TRASH

HEY, BUDDY, YOU FORGOT SOMETHING. LITTERING IS A CRIME, YOU KNOW.

HUH? WHAT IS SHE DOING?

TRA

REALLY?!

TOSS

TRAS

GOOD EVENING, LADIES AND GENTLEMEN.

WHO'S THAT?

MAYBE HE'S A LUMBERJACK?

ALLOW ME TO INTRODUCE MYSELF. MY REAL NAME IS RAMON AND MY CAMP NAME IS RAVEN.

I'VE BEEN WORKING BEHIND THE SCENES TO MAKE SURE THINGS RUN SMOOTHLY. I'M THE CAMP MEDIC, AND OUR RESIDENT STORYTELLER...

SO, WHO'S UP FOR A LITTLE GHOST STORY?

THIS IS THE STORY ABOUT A MINER WHO LOST HIS HEAD...

LIKE, HE LITERALLY LOST HIS HEAD.

HEH.

DO YOU REMEMBER THAT MINE YOU PASSED ON YOUR WAY IN?

JUST IMAGINE, SIXTY YEARS AGO, A CREW OF TWENTY MINERS WERE BLASTING THEIR WAY THROUGH A WALL OF SOLID ROCK.

THREE, TWO, ONE...

BLAM!

SOMETIMES THEY'D GET LUCKY AND FIND GOLD...

BUT THIS ONE TIME, THEY WERE NOT SO LUCKY...THERE WAS A CAVE-IN. TWENTY MINERS WENT IN AND ONLY NINETEEN CAME OUT.

WHAT DOES THAT TELL YOU? IF NINETEEN WERE SAFE, WHAT'S THE PROBLEM?

ONE WENT MISSING.

EXACTLY. WHEN THE SMOKE AND DUST SETTLED, THE MINERS WENT BACK INSIDE TO SEARCH FOR THEIR MISSING FRIEND.

Raven

AFTER DIGGING THROUGH THE DEBRIS, THEY UNCOVERED HIS FEET AND LEGS. THEY PULLED AND PULLED TO FREE THEIR FRIEND...

THEY RECOVERED HIS BODY BUT NOT THE HEAD. IN FACT, THEY NEVER FOUND IT.

GASP!

AND IT'S STILL IN THERE TODAY.

NO HEAD!

FOLKS SAY YOU CAN HEAR HIS VOICE CALLING OUT FOR HELP ON SPECIAL FALL NIGHTS WHEN THE AIR IS COLD AND STILL...ON NIGHTS JUST LIKE TONIGHT.

THE END.

THANK YOU AND GOOD NIGHT. SWEET DREAMS, CAMPERS. PLEASE LOOK TO YOUR TEACHERS AND CHAPERONES.

CLAP CLAP

WOO-HOO!

MY CLASS, OVER HERE.

MR. WOLF, WAS THAT A TRUE STORY? I THINK I'M GOING TO HAVE NIGHTMARES.

I WASN'T SCARED.

BRR. IT'S GETTING COLD!

NO, PENNY. IT WAS ALL MADE UP.

SOME PARTS WERE REAL.

I THINK IT'S REAL. IT'S ALL TERRIBLY REAL.

ALL RIGHT. IT'S LATE AND WE NEED TO BE GETTING TO BED ASAP*. I'M SURE YOU'RE ALL EXHAUSTED.

I FEEL LIKE I'M GOING TO BARF.

YAWN

GOOD NIGHT, YOU ALL. THE JOY OF DAWN AWAITS US IN THE MORNING.

GOOD NIGHT!

SEE YOU TOMORROW.

OH, IS DAWN YOUR REAL NAME?

NEGATIVE. BUT GOOD GUESS.

IS IT BARBARA, BETTY, BEYONCÉ?

YOU'VE ALREADY USED UP YOUR GUESSES, BANANA SLUG.

OKAY, PLEASE FOLLOW YOUR CHAPERONES TO THE CABINS. SLEEP TIGHT.

*AS SOON AS POSSIBLE

117

CHAPTER EIGHT

Surprise

YOU JUST LOOK SO HAPPY NOW. YOU'VE BEEN GRUMPY ALL DAY.

THAT'S BECAUSE I MADE A NEW FRIEND.

HELLO PUPPY®

IS THERE ANYTHING BETTER THAN A GOOD BOOK?

SKY world

LIGHTS OUT, LADIES!

THE HEADLESS MINER.

CAN'T WE READ, GI-GI?

HELLO PUP

GOOD NIGHT.

GROAN

G'NITE.

121

YAWN

I NEED TO PEE SO BADLY.

YAWN!

IT'S SO QUIET.

BRRR

COLD! COLD! COLD!

IT'S SNOWING!

I CAN'T BELIEVE IT!

WAHOO!

CHIPMUNK TRACKS?

SNOW! SNOW! SNOW!

I CALLED YOUR PARENTS, RATTLE-SNAKE, BUT THEY DIDN'T ANSWER. ARE YOU SURE YOU FEEL WELL ENOUGH TO PARTICIPATE?

YEAH, I THINK I'LL BE OKAY.

POOR KID!

YOU HAVE RATS IN YOUR SCHOOL?

THEY'RE MY FRIENDS.

MO-OM!

DISHES

TRASH

COMPOST

HEY!

MARGOT, CATCH!

GRR.

SORRY!

FOR THE LAST TIME, MY NAME IS CLOVER!

EEEEK!

LET'S GET EM!

THIS IS GOOD. LET THEM GET THEIR ENERGY OUT.

BWAAA! BWAAA!

MR. WOLF!

I SPOKE TOO SOON.

SOB! BOO-HOO!

IT WAS THOSE BIG KIDS FROM THE OTHER SCHOOL.

THEY'RE CALLED BUZZ SAW AND PITCHFORK.

HE GOT HIT IN THE FACE.

ALL RIGHT, EVERYONE. SNOWBALL FIGHT'S OVER! COME ON BACK!

SAME GOES FOR MY CLASS.

WHAT?!

BUT WE WERE HAVING FUN.

POK!

HOW ARE YOU FEELING?

NOT GREAT, BUT I'LL LIVE.

HAVE YOU SEEN MY SOCCER BALL?

NO, BUT LOOK. PITCHFORK AND BUZZ SAW GOT IN TROUBLE.

HEY, WOLVERINE, I'M SORRY I HIT YOU IN THE FACE.

THAT'S OKAY.

YEAH... SORRY.

I THINK YOUR NAME IS COOL, BY THE WAY.

THANKS.

COME ON, BOBBY.

ROLL

ROLL

CIRCLE UP, EVERYONE.

HI, HUCKLEBERRY.

CHAPTER NINE
A Rare Sight

A VISIT TO THE NURSERY

EVERYONE GETS TO TAKE HOME A TREE WE GREW HERE IN THE NURSERY.

WHO CAN TELL US WHY TREES ARE SO IMPORTANT?...YES, LI'L CRAWDAD?

TREES GIVE US FOOD, LIKE FRUITS, SEEDS, AND LEAVES. THEY ALSO PROVIDE SHELTER FOR MANY ANIMALS.

RIGHT! FOOD AND SHELTER. MANY BIRD SPECIES SUCH AS EAGLES, OSPREY, RAVENS, AND OWLS NEED TREES TO HOLD UP THEIR NESTS.

FOREST LAYERS

Emergent layer

Canopy

Understory

Undergrowth

DO YOU THINK WE'LL SEE ANY EAGLES WHILE WE'RE HERE?

WE MIGHT. THERE IS A BALD EAGLE, BUT IT HASN'T BEEN SPOTTED FOR A FEW WEEKS. WE'LL JUST HAVE TO KEEP OUR EYES PEELED.

SO, WHAT MORE DO WE KNOW ABOUT THE IMPORTANCE OF TREES?

*CARBON DIOXIDE

ALL THAT EXTRA CARBON IN THE ATMOSPHERE IS HEATING UP OUR PLANET AND IT'S MAKING OUR CLIMATE UNSTABLE. THAT'S WHAT WE CALL CLIMATE CHANGE, OR GLOBAL WARMING.

THE GREENHOUSE EFFECT
CO_2 and other greenhouse gases trap the heat in our atmosphere

SUN
EARTH
ATMOSPHERE

BUT WE CAN DO SOMETHING ABOUT IT BY USING LESS FOSSIL FUELS AND PROTECTING OUR FORESTS.

EACH OF YOU HAVE YOUR VERY OWN TOOL TO FIGHT CLIMATE CHANGE. PLANT A TREE TO SAVE OUR FUTURE! RAISE YOUR HAND IF YOU'RE READY TO FIGHT GLOBAL WARMING.

I AM!

YEAH!

I AM!

WE HAVE TO!

FOR SURE!

YES!

OF COURSE!

ME!

AND NOW, EVERYONE, WE'RE GOING TO GET READY FOR OUR NEXT AND FINAL ACTIVITY...A HIKE UP HORSE THIEF MOUNTAIN FOR THE MOST BEAUTIFUL VIEW YOU'VE EVER SEEN.

AND IT'LL BE YOUR LAST CHANCE TO GUESS MY NAME.

YES, BUMBLEBEE?

IS YOUR NAME PHOTOSYNTHESIS?

HA!... TRY AGAIN.

OXYGEN? CO_2?

DRIP

DRIP

DROP

SO, ARE YOU GOING TO FINALLY TELL ME WHAT HAPPENED WITH YOU AND AZIZA?

I TOLD YOU WE HAD A LITTLE DISAGREEMENT.

JUST TELL ME, ALREADY.

OKAY, I WILL. WAIT UP.

MR. WOLF, I'M HOT.

WELL, WHY DON'T YOU TAKE YOUR JACKET OFF? THAT'S WHAT I DID.

OH, FINE.

AH! THAT FEELS SO MUCH BETTER!

STOP MOVING, BUMBLEBEE.

BUT IT TICKLES!

WATER BREAK.

WHERE'S YOUR BOW TIE, STEWART?

IT GOT DIRTY.

NO EATING, PLEASE. WE'LL HAVE OUR LUNCHES WHEN WE REACH THE TOP.

AW!

KEEP IT UP! WE'RE ALMOST TO THE SUMMIT. WHEN WE GET THERE, YOU WILL ALL SMILE WITH JOY!

HUFF

NOW WE CAN EAT. WHAT A JOY THIS DAY HAS BEEN.

YAY! I'M STARVING!

IS YOUR REAL NAME JOY?

BINGO!

THUNDER EGG'S THE WINNER!... GOOD LISTENING.

NICE ONE, MIGUEL.

DID SHE SAY HER REAL NAME IS BINGO?

SOMEONE GOT THEIR APPETITE BACK.

MMHMM.

...AND THEN I ELBOWED HER IN THE FACE BY ACCIDENT. NOW SHE HATES ME AND IT'S ALL MY FAULT.

SOB

I CAN SEE WHY SHE'D BE MAD AT YOU, BUT I'M SURE SHE DOESN'T HATE YOU...ARE YOU FAKE CRYING?

NO, THIS IS JUST HOW I CRY.

HA HA

YOU LAUGH WHEN YOU CRY?

SOMETIMES.

JUST WALK UP TO AZIZA AND TELL HER YOU'RE SORRY.

BUT I DON'T KNOW HOW.

IT'S EASY. YOU JUST SAY, "I'M SORRY." COME ON, BANANA SLUG.

YOU CAN FIX THIS.

UP ON YOUR FEET, LITTLE SLUGGY. LET'S GET OUR FRIEND BACK.

OKAY, FINE.

SNIFF

NOW I'M SHIVERING.

THEN PUT YOUR JACKET BACK ON.

GOOD GRIEF!

BRRR

AZIZA...I'M SORRY?

SAY IT LIKE YOU MEAN IT, RANDY.

...AND WHAT ARE YOU SORRY FOR?

OKAY, OKAY...I'M SORRY... FOR ELBOWING YOU IN THE FACE...

AND I'M SORRY FOR BEING SO BOSSY...THERE, I SAID IT.

GOOD JOB, RANDY.

WHAT IS GOING ON HERE?

APOLOGY ACCEPTED.

PHEW

SHAKE HANDS, BANANA SLUG.

FRIENDS?

FRIENDS!

YAY!

DID ZI-ZI ASK IF YOU LIKED *HAZELTON THE MUSICAL* YET?

SHAKE

I'D NEVER HEARD OF IT BEFORE, BUT AZIZA LET ME LISTEN TO IT YESTERDAY IN HER CABIN. I LOVED IT!

WELL, IF YOU DIDN'T ALREADY LIKE IT, AZIZA WOULD BUG YOU ABOUT IT OVER AND OVER.

MOVE OVER.

AZIZA'S OBSESSED WITH ALEXANDER HAZELTON.

TRUE!

NOD

I ONCE WROTE A RESEARCH PAPER ON ALEXANDER HAZELTON, AND MR. WOLF SAID IT WAS TOO LONG.

WHAT?! HOW COULD A PAPER BE TOO LONG?

EXACTLY!

STILL, NONE OF THE NAMES I CAN THINK OF FEEL RIGHT.

FLOWER, DAISY, BUTTERCUP, DIXIE CUP? NOPE.

PETUNIA, ROSE, LAVENDER, STRAWBERRY, LIZARD, LICHEN? NONE OF THEM FIT ME.

IT WAS SO EASY FOR EVERYONE ELSE.

LET'S SING MUSIC FROM *HAZELTON*.

♪ ♫ ♩ ♫

CHAPTER TEN
Good-bye

SWEEP
SWEEP

ROLL

NO WAY! HUCKLEBERRY GAVE YOU A REAL THUNDER EGG?

CAN I SEE?

MOP

Important phone #s

Randy (BFF) 555-7421
Penny 555-8646
Lola 555-5618
Oscar (science fair) 555-1373
Hafiza (cousin) 555-1589
Margot 555-2468
Natasha (fawn) 5

AZIZA'S
KEEP
OUT!

I GUESS THAT HIKE WAS OPTIONAL FOR THEIR CLASS.

THEY WEREN'T IN TROUBLE?

NO, AND LOOK. THEY GAVE ME THEIR PHONE NUMBERS.

NO WAY!

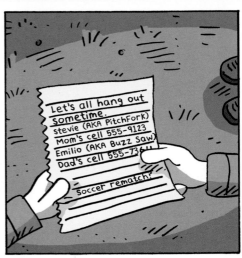

Let's all hang out sometime.
stevie (AKA PitchFork)
Mom's cell 555-9123
Emilio (AKA Buzz Saw)
Dad's cell 555-73...

Soccer rematch!

THEIR REAL NAMES ARE...

STEVIE AND EMILIO!

HUH!

DID YOU TELL THEM OURS?

OOPS! I FORGOT TO.

WHO CAN TELL ME ONE THING YOU LEARNED DURING YOUR STAY AT BATTLE AX CREEK?

YES, BUMBLE-BEE?

I LEARNED THAT PLANTS GIVE US OXYGEN AND MAKE THEIR OWN FOOD FROM THE SUN, CARBON DIOXIDE, AND WATER.

YES, THAT'S PHOTOSYNTHESIS.

WHAT MORE DID WE LEARN? YES?

I LEARNED ABOUT HYDROELECTRICITY.

I LEARNED THAT NATASHA DOESN'T HAVE ANY FRIENDS IN HER CLASS, AND IT MAKES ME SO SAD.

YEAH, BUT SHE HAS US NOW. AND WE'LL ALL BE IN THE SAME MIDDLE SCHOOL IN A COUPLE OF YEARS.

BUT THAT'S SO LONG!

WE MADE IT!

FINALLY!

PLEASE USE THE RESTROOM IF YOU NEED TO.

BYE, EAGLE EYE! THANK YOU FOR COMING.

ACK! P.U.!

TAKE A SEAT. I NEED TO COUNT EVERYONE.

Thank you to . . .

Ariel, Marlen, Don, Alona, Lisa, David, Ed, Jeremy, Anna, Elisha, Theo, Miles, Elliott, Gena, Justin, Elizabeth, Briceton, Benjamin, Derrik, Kristen, Sharon, Joe, and all my extended family.

My agent, Judy Hansen, my editor, Cassandra Pelham Fulton, Jordana Kulak, David Saylor, Phil Falco, Lizette Serrano, Shivana Sookdeo, and everyone at Scholastic who has worked behind the scenes to support Mr. Wolf's class.

Saadia Faruqi, for reading early drafts and giving me invaluable feedback. Please check out her fantastic Yasmin book series.

Dav Pilkey, Raina Telgemeier, Greg Means, Jonathan Hill, Lark Pien, Jess Keating, Vera Brosgol, Breena Bard, Thien Pham, Gene Luen Yang, Jarrett Lerner, John Schu, Kate Messner, and Jim Di Bartolo for your support.

My students, as always: You inspire me, challenge me, and keep me grounded. You are the future.

Tom Spurgeon and The Comics Reporter for building and supporting a community of cartoonists and comics readers. You are missed.

Alec Longstreth for his amazing coloring job and his wife, Claire Sanders, for assisting. Please check out Alec's comics at isleofelsi.com.

And finally, thank you, dear reader, for spending time in Mr. Wolf's class. This book wouldn't exist without you.

Author photo by Renée Lopez

Aron Nels Steinke is the Eisner Award–winning creator of the Mr. Wolf's Class series, and is the illustrator and coauthor, with Ariel Cohn, of *The Zoo Box*. He teaches fourth and fifth grade in Portland, Oregon, to a group of students who are much too competitive at four square. Aron's favorite wild berry is the thimbleberry (*Rubus parviflorus*), and he enjoys foraging for wild plants. The old-growth forest in this story was inspired by many places he likes to visit in the Pacific Northwest, such as the Opal Creek Wilderness area, Breitenbush Hot Springs, Oxbow Regional Park, and the Olympic National Forest. Visit Aron online at mrwolfsclass.com.

Don't stop now! Check out these other
exciting adventures in Mr. Wolf's class!